DANIEL TIGER'S NEIGHBORHOOD

DANIEL'S LITTLE SONGS

FOR BIG FEELINGS

Adapted by May Nakamura
Poses and layouts by Jason Fruchter

Simon Spotlight
New York   London   Toronto   Sydney   New Delhi

SIMON SPOTLIGHT

An imprint of Simon & Schuster Children's Publishing Division

1230 Avenue of the Americas, New York, New York 10020

This Simon Spotlight edition August 2020

© 2020 The Fred Rogers Company

Adapted from the screenplays written by Kevin Monk, Jill Cozza Turner, Jennifer Hamburg, Alexandra Cassel, Melinda LaRose, Dan Yaccarino, Wendy Harris, Becky Friedman, Angela C. Santomero, Dustin Ferrer, Syndi Shumer, Leah Gotcsik, and Jack Rowley Jr.
SIMON SPOTLIGHT and colophon are registered trademarks of Simon & Schuster, Inc.

For information about special discounts for bulk purchases, please contact Simon & Schuster Special Sales at 1-866-506-1949 or business@simonandschuster.com.

Manufactured in China 0620 SCP

2 4 6 8 10 9 7 5 3 1

ISBN 978-1-5344-7090-3 • ISBN 978-1-5344-7091-0 (eBook)

TABLE OF CONTENTS

Hi, neighbor! It's me, Daniel Tiger.

Wherever I go and whatever I do, I always like to sing! When I'm happy, I sing a song to share my happy feelings with my friends and family. When I'm angry, singing helps me remember to take a deep breath and count to four. What kind of songs do you like to sing? Who do you like to sing with?

It's time to sing!

For grown-ups:

In this book there are more than fifty songs that you can sing any time you need them. Each song comes with a short story that you can read with your child about a time that it helped Daniel with his feelings. There are also tips and hints written especially for you.

NEW EXPERIENCES

New experiences can be very exciting, but sometimes they can make you feel nervous, too. Whether you're visiting a new place or eating a new food, these songs will help you feel ready to try something new!

When we do something new, let's talk about what we'll do!

Sing this song before your first:
• dentist, doctor, or haircut appointment
• day of school
• visit to a new place
• bus, plane, train, or boat ride

Daniel has a checkup with his new dentist, Dr. Plat. She shows him all her dentist's tools and says that she will look inside his mouth to check if his teeth are healthy. Once he knows what will happen during the checkup, Daniel doesn't feel nervous anymore!

Helpful hints for grown-ups:

• Encourage your child to ask questions about the new experience. It's okay if you don't know all the answers.
• Be honest with your child, even if that means telling them that a shot will probably hurt a little bit. It will give your child more time to think and prepare rather than being surprised in the moment.
• Play pretend with your child, acting out what might happen during the new experience. It will help them feel in control and understand what to expect.
• After the experience, talk again with your child about what happened. How did they feel? Was there anything surprising about the experience?

Wherever you go, you can find something you know to help you feel better!

Sing this song when you're:
- visiting a new place
- starting at a new school
- moving to a new home

Jodi Platypus is new to the neighborhood. On the first day of school, she feels shy and nervous to meet new classmates. Then she sees her neighbor Daniel. She's played with him before! Seeing someone she knows makes Jodi feel better.

Helpful hints for grown-ups:

• Take time to point out things about your new home, town, or your child's new school that are familiar to your child. It might be a familiar store, a plant growing in the yard, or a toy in the play area at school.
• When you're packing, put some of your child's toys near the top of the boxes. Then your child will have something familiar and comforting to play with when you unpack.
• If possible, plan for you and your child to tour the new school and meet the teacher before the first day.

If something seems hard to do,
try it a little bit at a time!

Sing this song when you're:

• trying something new, like a sport or a game

• learning something new at school

• doing something difficult

Daniel is going ice-skating for the first time, but he's not sure if he wants to try it. It looks so hard! Dad Tiger helps Daniel onto the ice rink a little bit at a time. First, Daniel bends his knees. Then he looks straight ahead and marches his feet. Pretty soon, Daniel knows how to ice-skate . . . and it doesn't feel so hard anymore!

Helpful hints for grown-ups:

• Brand-new experiences can feel especially overwhelming to children. Breaking up the experience into many small steps will make it seem less daunting for your child.

• When your child is trying something new, it's okay to take breaks. They don't need to accomplish something new in one sitting.

• If your child is adamant about not trying something new, there's no need to force it. They might not feel ready now, but they might feel more ready the next day or the next time.

When something is new, holding a hand can help you!

Sing this song when you're:
- trying something new
- visiting a new place
- meeting someone new

Daniel and Margaret are seeing a fireworks show for the first time. They feel a little nervous about the loud noise. When they hold each other's hands, though, they start feeling better. Daniel discovers that fireworks are bright, sparkly, and beautiful!

Helpful hints for grown-ups:

• Holding your child's hand is a reminder that they're not alone in facing a new experience. Your touch provides your child with support and encouragement.
• When something is new, your child will look to you for your reaction. If you look calm and relaxed, it shows your child that they can feel relaxed too.
• You can sing this song even if an experience is new for you, too. You can give and receive comfort at the same time.

With a little help, you can be brave!

Sing this song when:
• you're trying something new
• you're feeling nervous or scared

At his first gymnastics class, Daniel feels nervous and scared of walking on the balance beam. Henrietta Pussycat holds his hand to help him while he walks across. Soon, Daniel feels brave enough to walk on the balance beam on his own!

Helpful hints for grown-ups:

• Talk about what your child can expect to happen. You might be able to provide information that calms their fears, especially if they have a misconception or misunderstanding of what might happen.
• If your child is afraid of doing something new, they don't need to be brave enough to do everything at once. You can help them be brave little by little.
• Reassure your child that being brave doesn't have to happen all on their own—you or another grown-up will be there to help. Knowing that they have support from someone will help your child gain confidence.

15

Try a new food,
it might taste good!

Sing this song when you're:

- trying a food for the first time
- visiting a new restaurant

Miss Elaina and Daniel are having a playdate. For dinner, Mom Tiger cooks something new called veggie spaghetti. Daniel isn't sure he wants to try it. What if he doesn't like it? But then he takes a little bite . . . and he likes it! The spaghetti tastes so good that he finishes his whole plate. Daniel is happy that he tried something new!

Helpful hints for grown-ups:

• Reassure your child that it's okay to not like the food. What's important is giving it a try!
• Invite your child to help prepare meals in the kitchen. They may be more interested in trying foods that they helped you cook.
• Exposing your child to a variety of different foods and flavors will help them grow stronger and stay healthy.
• When your child is trying a new food, give them a small serving at first. Seeing a plate full of new food might be overwhelming.

When you wonder, you can try to find out more!

Sing this song when:

- you're exploring outside
- you're learning something new at school
- you've seen something that you've never seen before
- you have a question . . . about anything!

Daniel and Prince Wednesday are outside playing with a lizard named Nellie. Suddenly Nellie disappears! Where did she go? Daniel and Prince Wednesday look at a book and learn that some lizards can change color. Then they go back outside and find Nellie turning from brown to green as she enters the grass. That's rrroyally neat!

Helpful hints for grown-ups:

• Offer ways for your child to find out more about a question they have or a topic that interests them. You can look at books or online for more information. A magnifying glass, binoculars, or a telescope can also help your child take a closer look.

• Your child doesn't need to go into the countryside in order to experience nature. They can learn so much just by being outside in a park, on the sidewalk, or looking up at the sky.

• Choose a tree or a plant to observe with your child over time. How do the colors change with the season? Does it look different based on the weather?

*You can change your hair,
or what you wear,
but no matter what you do,
you're still you!*

Sing this song when:

• you're wearing new clothes, shoes, or accessories

• you get a haircut

20

Daniel's favorite red sweater is in the wash, which means that he can't wear it today. Prince Wednesday's glasses need to be fixed, so he looks a little different today too. No matter what they look like, Prince Wednesday is still the same rrroyally silly prince and Daniel is still the kind, imaginative tiger on the inside!

Helpful hints for grown-ups:

- Young children are still developing their self-awareness and identity. Some children really believe that if they wear a costume or change their appearance, they turn into someone or something else!
- Any kind of change, even a simple haircut, can be a big deal for children. Reassure your child that no matter what changes, they're still the same person on the inside.
- Tell family stories or memories of when your child was younger. Sharing these stories will help your child understand more about themselves and develop a sense of self-identity.

BIG FEELINGS

Everyone feels a lot of different feelings, and that's okay! Talking and singing about how you feel will help you manage and express your feelings.

 Give a squeeze, nice and slow, take a deep breath, and let it go.

Sing this song when:
- you're having trouble sitting still
- you need to calm down or pay attention
- you're feeling too silly or excited in a place where you need to be calm

Prince Wednesday is so excited for storytime at the library that it's hard to sit still! It's okay to be silly sometimes, but at a quiet library, Prince Wednesday needs to be calm. He wraps his arms around himself and gives himself a nice, slow squeeze. Then he takes a deep breath and slowly lets it out. After that, Prince Wednesday feels less silly, and he is able to stay calm and listen to the story.

Helpful hints for grown-ups:

• Calming down takes practice. Show your child how to take slow, deep breaths.
• Play games like freeze tag, which help children understand that sometimes they can be silly and sometimes they must sit still.
• If your child is feeling too silly to give themselves a squeeze, you can also give them a hug to help them

It's okay to feel sad sometimes.
Little by little, you'll feel better again!

Sing this song when:
- something sad happens
- you feel left out
- you're having a bad day

Daniel wants to play with Katerina and O the Owl, but it's time for dinner. He feels sad because his friends are playing without him. Dad Tiger gives Daniel a hug and tells him that it's okay to feel sad sometimes. Daniel eats a yummy dinner with Mom and Dad Tiger. Then he talks about his sad feelings and gets another hug. Little by little, Daniel starts to feel better again!

Helpful hints for grown-ups:

• Activities like drawing, talking, or hugging a stuffed animal can help comfort your child when they're feeling sad.
• Take deep breaths with your child to help them relax.
• Sometimes it's not possible to fix everything that makes your child sad. But you can still listen to show that you care when your child talks about their feelings.

*Ask questions about
what happened.
It might help.*

Sing this song when:

• your pet or someone else you know dies

• something bad happens at home, at school, or on the news

Daniel loves his pet Blue Fish. One day Blue Fish dies—that means it can't breathe, swim, or play anymore. Daniel feels sad, so he asks a lot of questions and draws a picture to help him understand what happened. Blue Fish might not be alive anymore, but with his picture, Daniel will be able to always remember his pet.

Helpful hints for grown-ups:

• Encourage your child to ask questions. Some of the questions, or the repetitiveness of the questions, might feel surprising, but talking through the death will help your child understand and accept what happened.
• Don't be afraid to show your own emotions too. If you feel sad, tell your child how you're feeling. It will encourage them to express their emotions to you too.
• When something tragic happens at school or on the news, encourage your child to talk about it. You can help clarify misunderstandings, or even rumors, that they might have heard.

*When you feel so mad
that you want to roar,
take a deep breath and count to 4.
1...2...3...4...*

Sing this song when:

• you're mad or you think something is unfair

• you don't get what you want

28

Daniel and his friends are picking instruments to play at Music Man Stan's shop. When Katerina doesn't get to play the triangle, she feels so MAD! Then she takes a deep breath and counts to four. It helps her calm down. Now Katerina feels ready to wait her turn until she can play the triangle.

Helpful hints for grown-ups:

• Encourage your child to use words to describe why they're mad.
• You can also help your child release their angry energy by running, dancing, or doing other physical activities.
• Do something fun, like singing a song or making a silly face, to help ease your child's anger.
• Remind your child that it's okay to feel mad sometimes. Everyone does! But mad feelings can go away with time and by taking deep breaths.

Stop, stop, stop yourself!
It's okay to be angry.
It's not okay to hurt someone.

Sing this song when:

• you're angry

• you feel like hitting, biting, throwing, or pushing

When Daniel gets angry at Miss Elaina for taking his seat, he almost pushes her—until he stops himself and remembers that it's okay to be mad, but it's not okay to hit someone. He feels proud for knowing when to stop.

Helpful hints for grown-ups:

• Offer other solutions for your child to release their anger, like taking deep breaths and using their words.
• Encourage your child to try to imagine being in the other person's shoes. You can ask questions like, "Have you been pushed before? How did it feel?"
• Play games that help your child practice physical self-control, like freeze dance or freeze tag.

Use your words!

Sing this song when:

• you're frustrated or upset

• you're having trouble expressing how you feel

Daniel and Katerina are playing "train." When Katerina decides to be the train engineer, Daniel gets upset. Katerina doesn't know what's wrong until Daniel says that *he* wanted to be train engineer. Then she agrees to be the caboose instead. Daniel learns that it's important to use your words and say what you're feeling!

Helpful hints for grown-ups:

- When children feel a strong emotion, they sometimes stop communicating. It's important to tell your child that words are the best way to say what's wrong.
- Tell your child, "I can see that you're upset, but it's hard for me to help you if I don't know why."
- It can be difficult to have a learning moment in the middle of a tantrum. Instead, have conversations about identifying emotions—and how to best express them—when your child is feeling calmer and ready to listen.
- Praise your child when they use their words to communicate when they're upset.

♪ ♫ **When you're feeling frustrated, take a step back and ask for help!** ♫ ♪

Sing this song when:

• you feel frustrated

• something isn't going the way you want it to

Daniel wants Tigey to sit on top of the block castle that he built. No matter how hard he tries, Tigey and his blocks keep tumbling down. Daniel feels frustrated, so he takes a step back and asks Mom Tiger to help him. Together, they rebuild the castle so Tigey can stay up on top. All Daniel needed was a little bit of help!

Helpful hints for grown-ups:

• Help your child make the connection between their body and their emotions. Do they feel their heart beating fast or their muscles tightening? That might mean that they're feeling frustrated and need to take a step back.
• Teach your child to not give up when they feel frustrated. Instead, they can ask for help.
• Supporting your child while they try again will make them feel more confident and ready to succeed.

When you feel jealous, talk about it and we'll figure something out!

Sing this song when:
- you feel jealous
- you want a toy that someone else has
- you feel like someone else is getting more attention than you

Daniel, Katerina, and O the Owl are playing with O's new bubble wand. When it's time for Katerina to go home, she doesn't want to give the wand back. She feels jealous of O and wants the toy for herself! Katerina tells O and her mom how she feels. They all decide that they can play again with the wand next time they play together. After talking about her feelings, Katerina feels better!

Helpful hints for grown-ups:

• Having the words to describe emotions, such as jealousy, will help your child talk about them.
• Brainstorm with your child about ways to feel less jealous. If your child is jealous of a friend's toy, they could ask the friend to play together. You can also help them focus on the positive: they have a kind friend who will share their toy, and your child also has toys of their own that they love to play with.
• Spend regular one-on-one time with your child. When your child generally feels secure about receiving your attention, they may be less likely to feel jealous and act out when you're focused on something else.

*Sometimes you feel two feelings
at the same time,
and that's okay!*

Sing this song when:

- you feel different feelings at once
- you're feeling nervous

Daniel is at the neighborhood carnival, but he feels kind of mixed-up about riding the Ferris wheel. He feels excited, but he feels a little scared, too. Mom Tiger says that it's okay to feel more than one feeling at the same time. Daniel decides not to ride the Ferris wheel until he feels less scared and more excited.

Helpful hints for grown-ups:

- It's easy for children to have mixed feelings about something, especially a new experience. Reassure your child that feeling more than one thing is natural.
- When your child feels mixed-up, encourage them to talk through all the different emotions they're feeling. This demonstrates that each and every feeling is important.
- Tell your child that if they feel conflicted about something, it's okay to not decide what they want to do right away. With more time and information, some of the nervous or scared feelings might fade away.

When something seems bad, turn it around and find something good!

Sing this song when:

- something unexpected happens
- rainy or stormy weather gets in the way of playtime
- you accidentally break a toy and can't play with it anymore

Daniel, Prince Wednesday, and Miss Elaina are having a picnic outside, but then it starts to rain. At first they are disappointed, but then they try to find something else fun to do. Daniel, Prince Wednesday, and Miss Elaina decide to have the picnic inside the clock factory instead. Indoor picnics are grr-ific too!

Helpful hints for grown-ups:

• Sometimes things don't turn out the way we want. It's important for your child to know that an unexpected event isn't always a bad thing.

• Help manage your child's expectations. Distinguish between something that will definitely happen, such as participating in a game, and something that might or might not happen, like winning the game.

• Ask questions like: "What did you wish had happened? Why do you think it didn't happen?" These questions will help your child problem-solve and think of ways to turn something disappointing into

*This is my happy song,
and I could sing it all day long!*

Sing this song when:

- you're happy and you want to share it with others!

42

It's a beautiful day in the neighborhood! Daniel feels so happy to be riding Trolley with Mom Tiger. As they ride, they decide to sing a song together. Daniel loves to sing and do other things that make him happy!

Helpful hints for grown-ups:

• Celebrate the small things that make you and your child happy, like going to the bakery or the playground.
• Have conversations with your child about what made them happy that day. You can start by sharing something that made you happy.
• Encourage your child to share and spread their happiness with others. Saying hello, making a gift, or doing

TAKING CARE OF YOUR BODY

Taking care of your body is important for you to stay healthy and grow bigger. You can sing these songs throughout the day, from when you wake up to when you go to bed.

Clothes on, eat breakfast,
brush teeth, put on shoes,
and off to school!

Sing this song when:
- you wake up in the morning
- you're getting ready for the day

Good morning! There's so much to do as Daniel gets ready for school. First, he changes out of his pj's and into his clothes. Then he eats breakfast and brushes his teeth. Last, he puts on his shoes before going outside. Now Daniel is ready for the day!

Helpful hints for grown-ups:

- Some children resist their daily routine simply because it's mandatory. Give your child small choices, such as choosing which sweater to wear. It will make them feel in control and more willing to follow the routine.
- Morning routines go smoother with a little bit of preparation the night before. Lay out clothes and pack backpacks. This way, you'll have fewer things to do in the busy mornings.
- Sing the song to yourself before leaving the house. Putting the morning routine into a song might also help

*Think about what
you're going to do,
then pick the clothes
that are right for you!*

Sing this song when:

- you're getting dressed in the morning
- you're planning to start a new activity, like painting or playing outside

It is snowing in the Neighborhood of Make-Believe, and Daniel is excited to play outside. First, Daniel must get dressed. Should he wear his swimsuit or his raincoat? He finally decides on a snowsuit, boots, hats, and mittens. Wearing his warm clothes, Daniel is able to have a lot of fun playing in the cold with Miss Elaina!

Helpful hints for grown-ups:

• Talk regularly with your child about the seasons and the weather. Learning to notice changes in weather will help your child dress appropriately.
• Play dress-up, and talk about why people wear certain uniforms. For example, firefighters wear long sleeves and long pants to protect them from fires. Chefs wear aprons to keep their clothes clean.
• Remind your child that there are many things to think about when choosing the right clothes, such as

When you have to go potty,
STOP and go right away.
Flush and wash and be on your way!

Do you have to go potty?
Maybe yes? Maybe no?
Why don't you sit and try to go?

Sing these songs:
• when you need to go potty
• before you leave the house
• before you get in the car or on a bus or train
• before going to bed

Before Daniel leaves the house, he always sits on the potty and tries to go . . . especially because there's no potty on Trolley. After he finishes, he wipes with toilet paper and flushes the potty. Then he washes his hands and dries them too. Knowing how to go to the potty makes Daniel feel proud!

Helpful hints for grown-ups:

• Children can get caught up in their play and ignore that they need to go potty. Remind them to always go to the potty right away. When they come back from the potty, they can start playing again!
• Encourage your child to try to go to the potty before leaving the house or going somewhere without a potty. Bladders can be emptied even before they are completely full.
• When potty accidents happen, give your child a task, like changing their clothes or putting dirty clothes in the washing machine. These kinds of tasks helps children understand that accidents create extra work and

Bath time, brush teeth, pj's, story and song, and off to bed!

Sing this song when:
- it's the end of the day
- you're getting ready for bed

After dinner, it's time for Daniel to get ready for bed. First, he gets in the bathtub and scrubs until he's all clean. Then, he brushes his teeth and changes into his pj's. Last, Daniel's parents read him a story and sing a song. Goodnight, Daniel!

Helpful hints for grown-ups:

• If possible, give you and your child plenty of time for the bedtime routine. That way, you can get through all the steps without your child getting too sleepy and cranky.
• Having a routine at the end of the day helps your child get a good night's sleep. Going through the familiar actions will signal to their body that it's time to wind down.
• Make a bedtime routine that works best for you and your child. Your bedtime routine might include talking

We can take care of each other!

Sing this song when:

- you, a family member, or a friend is sick
- you are looking after your younger sibling
- you see someone who might need help

When Daniel eats a peach for the first time, his face and legs start to itch. His tummy hurts too. Dr. Anna says that Daniel has a peach allergy, which means that his body doesn't like peaches. She gives him medicine and tells him not to eat any more peaches. Whenever something is wrong, Doctor Anna is there to help Daniel feel better!

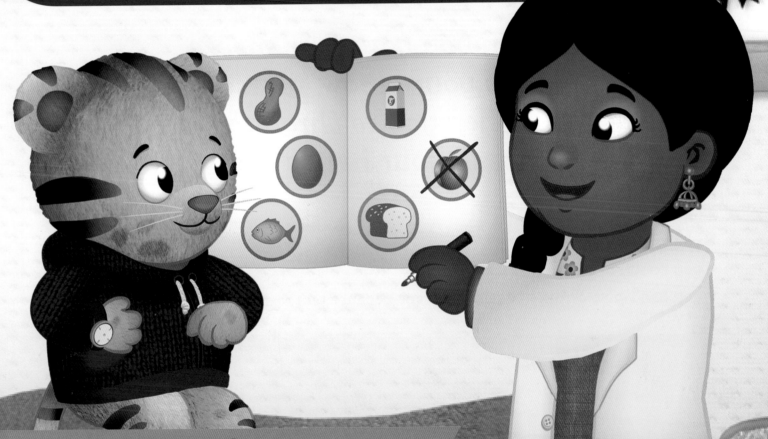

Helpful hints for grown-ups:

- Remind your child to always tell a grown-up right away if something hurts or they don't feel well.
- It's not easy to have an allergy or another health condition, but reassure your child that there are many people who can take care of them.
- Make a list of grown-ups that your child can go to for help when they need it: teachers, doctors, dentists, grandparents, and you.
- There are many ways your child can take care of other people. They can hold a younger sibling's hand when

When you're sick,
rest is best. Rest is best.

When you cough or sneeze,
use your elbow, please.
When you're through,
wash your hands too!

Sing these songs when:

- you're sick and not feeling well
- you cough or sneeze
- you can't play or have to miss an event because you're sick

Today is Prince Wednesday's birthday celebration at school, but Daniel feels sick. He sneezes, coughs, and feels warm. Dad Tiger picks up Daniel and takes him home to rest. Daniel is sad to miss Prince Wednesday's birthday, but resting is important for Daniel's body to fight the germs.

Helpful hints for grown-ups:

• Remind your child that everyone gets sick sometimes, even you!
• It can be disappointing for kids to miss playtime or other events. Tell your child that rest is important to help them feel better sooner . . . and be able to play again sooner!
• Teach your child to help fight off germs by washing hands and keeping them out of their mouth and nose.
• If your child is sick, gently remind them of ways to keep their germs from spreading to their friends and family members. For example, they should cough or sneeze into their elbows; wash their hands; and not share

GROWING UP AND BEING INDEPENDENT

You are growing and learning new things every day. Sing these songs as you begin to do more things on your own, and you'll feel proud!

 *Grown-ups come back!*

Sing this song when:
- you're being dropped off at school
- your grown-up is traveling and not at home
- you have a babysitter

Daniel has arrived at school, and it's time for Dad Tiger to leave. But Daniel wants his dad to stay and play with him instead. Dad says that he'll come back to pick him up later. Sure enough, at the end of the day, Dad comes back to school to take Daniel home. It's not so bad when grown-ups leave because Daniel knows that grown-ups come back!

Helpful hints for grown-ups:

• Give your child a note, a bracelet, or something else that will remind your child of you and comfort them while you're gone.
• Create a tradition for saying goodbye, like doing a special handshake or saying "Ugga Mugga." Having a routine will help your child get used to saying goodbye.
• Make sure to say goodbye! Slipping away while your child is distracted will make them more anxious the next time you leave.

Everyone is big enough, big enough to do something!

Sing this song when:

- you want to help out
- you feel left out by older friends or family members
- you're too small or too young to do something you want to do

Daniel's dad is building a playhouse, and Daniel wants to help. He might not be able to use the grown-up tools, but he's big enough to hand the glue to his dad and paint the door. Daniel feels so proud for being big enough to help!

Helpful hints for grown-ups:

• Many young children feel helpless or left out because they can't do all the things that grown-ups or their older siblings can. Reassure your child that they are important, no matter how small they may be.
• Brainstorm things that your child can do well. It can be things that they can do better because they're smaller, like playing hide-and-seek, or it can be talents like building blocks and making you laugh.
• Give your child ways to help out around the house, even if they are simple things, like putting napkins out on the table or handing you laundry to fold. It will make your child feel proud and needed in the family.

Grr. Grr. Grr out loud. Keep on trying, and you'll feel proud!

Sing this song when:

- you're trying something new
- you can't get something right on your first try
- you're frustrated or feel like giving up

Daniel is learning how to ride a bike. He wiggles and wobbles. "*Grr, grr, grr* . . . riding a bike is so hard!" But Daniel keeps trying, and slowly, he starts to move forward! Daniel feels so proud that he can ride a bike now.

Helpful hints for grown-ups:

• When things don't work out right away, your child might get frustrated. *Grr*-ing out loud releases those emotions so they can try again.

• Emphasize the process and not just the accomplishment. For example, even if your child doesn't learn how to tie their shoe right away, congratulate them for spending time on it and practicing.

• It might seem easier or faster to jump in and do something for your child. But if you let your child learn and try things on their own, it will help them build self-confidence.

Do your best. Your best is the best for you!

Sing this song when:

• you're trying to do something difficult

• you're not sure how to do something

• you lose a game, race, or contest

Music Man Stan decorates his music shop for the Neighborhood Fall Festival. Then a strong gust of wind ruins all his work! Katerina, Miss Elaina, and Daniel offer to put up the decorations again. Instead of putting them up the exact same way as Music Man Stan, they do *their* best to make the decorations look beautiful. It is the greatest Fall Festival yet!

Helpful hints for grown-ups:

• Remind your child that everyone has different abilities. Even if they can't do something that someone else can, they can still be proud of doing their best.
• Praise your child for trying hard, even if the results aren't what they are striving for.
• Sometimes it's easy to fall into the mindset that there's only one correct way to do something. Remind your child that there is often more than one way to do something well!

*It's okay to make mistakes.
Try to fix them, and
learn from them too!*

Sing this song when:

• you make a mistake

• you accidentally make a mess or break something

• you get a question wrong at school

64

Daniel and Prince Wednesday are having fun baking cookies at Baker Aker's bakery. Prince Wednesday gets a little too silly and accidentally knocks over the milk. It spills all over the table! He fixes his mistake by wiping up the milk. Prince Wednesday learns that next time he should be more careful when baking.

Helpful hints for grown-ups:

• Tell your child that no one is perfect, and everyone makes mistakes . . . even you!
• Try not to get too frustrated or upset if your child makes a mistake. You want your child to continue trying new things, even if that means they might make more mistakes.
• Reframe the mistake as a "learning moment." Ask your child what they could do differently next time.

When grown-ups are busy
and can't play with you,
look around, look around
to find something to do!

Sing this song when:

- your parent or caregiver is busy with something
- you're visiting a grown-up at their job
- you're feeling bored

Daniel is joining Mom Tiger at work today. She is busy, so Daniel looks around for something to do. He decides to draw a picture and play with some cardboard boxes. Daniel has a lot of fun playing on his own!

Helpful hints for grown-ups:

• Playing on their own helps children learn how to make their own decisions and manage their own time.
• Make sure not to overschedule your child. When children become used to jumping from one structured activity to another, it makes it harder to know how to play freely on their own.
• Help your child brainstorm ways to play on their own. They can draw a picture, play pretend with dolls or toys, or look at a book.

Try to solve the problem yourself, and you'll feel proud!

Sing this song when you:

• don't agree with your friend about how to play

• have a problem, like you lost or broke a toy

Daniel and Prince Wednesday are playing at school. Daniel wants to wear a green sweater and pretend to be a space alien. But there's a problem. Prince Wednesday wants to be a space alien, too, and there's only one green sweater. Then Daniel realizes that they can wear it together! Daniel and Prince Wednesday feel proud of solving the problem on their own!

Helpful hints for grown-ups:

• Before going straight to a grown-up, encourage your child to ask the question, "Can I fix this myself?" But remind them that it's also always okay to ask for help when they need it, especially in an emergency.

• Encourage your child to do things that make them feel proud. Your child will learn that pride and self-worth come not only from a grown-up's praise, but also from inside.

• When your child has a disagreement with a friend, remind your child that talking through the problem is a great first step to solving it.

Families come in all different shapes and sizes. Sing these songs to celebrate your special family.

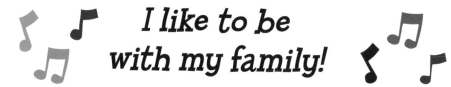

I like to be with my family!

Sing this song when:

- you're spending time with your family
- you want to show your family that you love them
- you're doing a special family tradition

Daniel likes to spend time with his dad, mom, and little sister. They play, eat dinner, and sing songs while they ride Trolley together. He also likes to visit Grandpere, who lives far away. Whenever they're together, Daniel and his family like to give each other big hugs and say, "Ugga Mugga!"

Helpful hints for grown-ups:

• Whenever possible, eat meals together as a family. Keep electronic devices away from the table and talk with one another about your days.

• Look at family photos and videos together. This way, your child can feel closer to family members that they don't see often.

• Create a family tradition. It can be as simple as going to the park every weekend or making a special family recipe together.

You can be a big helper in your family!

Sing this song when:

- you're taking care of a younger sibling
- you're helping with chores
- grown-ups look very busy and you want to help

When Daniel's little sister, Margaret, is born, Mom Tiger is very busy taking care of her. Daniel helps his mom change Margaret's diaper. When she starts crying, he shows her a book to make her calm down. Daniel feels so proud for helping out!

Helpful hints for grown-ups:

• Being a big helper gives your child a special role in the family, especially when they might be feeling insecure or worried about their place in the family after the arrival of another sibling.
• Taking care of the baby lets your older child feel proud of being an older sibling and less likely to feel jealous.
• Say "thank you" when your child helps out, even if the task isn't done perfectly. It will make your child more willing to help out in the future.

When a baby makes things different,
find a way to make things fun!

Sing this song when your:
- parent or caregiver is busy looking after your sibling
- little sibling wants to play with you

Daniel and his friends are marching in a pretend circus parade, but Margaret keeps following them around everywhere. At first Daniel only wants the parade to be for big kids, but then he lets his little sister be the funny clown in the parade! Things are different with a baby sister around, but "different" also means "more fun!"

Helpful hints for grown-ups:

• Turn the time spent taking care of a baby into a time for the whole family to be together. Provide fun ways for your older child to help with the baby, like singing or playing peekaboo.
• Don't forget to have one-on-one time with your older child. Even just a few minutes every day will mean a lot to them.

Families are different, and that's okay!

Sing this song when:
- you notice your family is different from someone else's family
- you are with your family

Daniel and his friends are having a "Dad and Me" campout. Katerina doesn't have a dad, so she goes to the campout with her mom. Katerina's mom says that families are all different, but what's important is that she loves Katerina very much! Katerina and her mom have a terrific time together at the campout!

Helpful hints for grown-ups:

• It's natural for your child to be curious and ask questions about other people's families. Talking about similarities and differences will help your child understand that differences aren't negatives.

• Remind your child that all families are different in many ways, from the number of people to how they spend time together. But families are all alike in that they look after one another.

• When your child is young, it's not important to explain the specifics of why families are different or how they came to be. It's enough to acknowledge the differences and accept them, and to remind your child of the similarities between your family and other families.

You can be mad at
someone you love.
When you are ready,
give them a hug!

Sing this song when:

• you're mad at someone you love, such as a family member or a friend

• someone you love is mad at you

Daniel and Dad are on their way to the post office when they walk past the playground. Daniel wants to play, but Dad says no. That makes Daniel so mad! He doesn't like being mad at his dad, since he loves him very much. Once he takes a deep breath and counts to four, he doesn't feel so mad anymore. Daniel and Dad give each other a hug and say, "I love you!"

Helpful hints for grown-ups:

- Remind your child that people don't need to be perfect to be loved.
- Some children are afraid of getting angry at a caregiver because they think they will lose that person's love. Reassure your child that you will still love them even when they are mad, and even when you are mad too.
- It's okay for your child to feel however they are feeling, even if that feeling is anger. What's important is that your child doesn't hurt other people with their anger.

FRIENDS AND NEIGHBORS

There are many ways to be a good friend and a kind neighbor. These songs will help you remember!

You can choose to be kind!

Sing this song when:

• you see someone who might want help

• you see someone who is sad

• you can be kind . . . which is anytime!

Daniel has a new friend named Chrissie, and they're pretending to be knights! Chrissie uses crutches and wears braces on her legs that help her walk. While Daniel runs around, Chrissie stands and guards the castle. She might sometimes need to play in a different way, but just like Daniel, Chrissie still loves to play!

Helpful hints for grown-ups:

• Sometimes grown-ups feel uncomfortable talking about people's differences, but it's common for children to be curious about people who are different from them. Having open conversations will help your child respect all people.

• It's just as important to talk about how your child is similar to other people. Some things that may be similar are hair color, hobbies and interests, or the language they speak at home.

• Remember that children with disabilities might sometimes need extra help, but they don't always want help. They like doing things on their own, too.

You can take a turn, and then I'll get it back!

Sing this song when:

- a friend or sibling wants to play with your toys
- you want to play on the same playground equipment as someone else

Prince Wednesday wants to play with Daniel's car. At first Daniel doesn't want to share, but then he lets Prince Wednesday take a turn. When Prince Wednesday is finished playing, he gives the car back to Daniel. Sharing makes playtime more fun for everyone!

Helpful hints for grown-ups:

• Reassure your child that "sharing" doesn't mean "giving away." They'll still get a toy back after their friend or sibling is finished playing with it.

• Use a timer to keep track of taking turns. That way, each child knows that they're getting a fair turn.

• Your child doesn't need to share everything, especially if it's a special toy. Before a playdate, put away the toys that are especially hard for your child to share.

Think about how someone else is feeling!

Sing this song when:

• you're feeling different feelings than someone else

• someone else is having a bad day and you don't understand why

• you're confused about how someone is acting

Chrissie has lost a very special bracelet, and she doesn't want to play with Daniel until she finds it. Teacher Harriet tells Daniel to use his empathy, and think about how Chrissie might be feeling. Once Daniel realizes that Chrissie is upset, he understands why she might not want to play with him anymore. Instead, he helps Chrissie find the bracelet!

Helpful hints for grown-ups:

• Children aren't born with empathy. It's something that they learn over time. Talking about empathy and what it means will help them learn to use empathy.

• Encourage empathy in your child by asking questions like "How do you think this person is feeling?" and "If you were them, how would you feel?"

• When children act or play pretend, they are putting themselves into other people's shoes and imagining what it's like to be someone else. Practicing these skills will help your child use them in real life.

Saying "I'm sorry" is the first step. Then "How can I help?"

Sing this song when:
- you've hurt someone's feelings
- you've made a mistake or done something wrong
- you want to help make up for something you've done

Prince Tuesday is upset because Daniel and Prince Wednesday took his crown without asking and got it dirty. Just saying "I'm sorry" doesn't make Prince Tuesday feel completely better, so Daniel and Prince Wednesday help fix their mistake by cleaning the sand off the crown. It's important to say sorry—and it's just as important to help make things better!

Helpful hints for grown-ups:

• Remind your child to say "I'm sorry" if they hurt someone else, even if they didn't mean to.
• Whether you or your child is apologizing, it's important to make eye contact. It shows your child that saying sorry is something to be done meaningfully and sincerely.
• When you make a mistake or lose your cool in front of your child, make sure to apologize. This shows children that everyone says sorry—and they also learn how it feels to receive an apology.
• Remind your child to do their best to help fix things or make the other person feel better. Taking this step will also help your child take responsibility for their actions.

89

Thank you for everything you do!

Sing this song:

- to someone you love
- when you want to say thank you
- when someone does something kind

It's Thank You Day in the neighborhood, and Grandpere is visiting. Daniel is sad that Grandpere isn't staying for the special party. Then he realizes that he can still be thankful for Grandpere's visit. And Grandpere thanks Daniel for all his big tiger hugs!

Helpful hints for grown-ups:

• Talk about all the people your child sees every day who they can thank: their teacher, crossing guard, siblings, and many others.
• Don't forget to thank your child, whether it's for helping you with a chore or just for being "them!" This will help your child understand how good it feels to receive thanks.
• Remind your child that there are many ways to show thanks. They can make a card or gift or give a hug.

PLAYTIME

Whether you're playing at home, at school, or on the playground, these songs will make playtime more fun!

When you wait, you can play, sing, or imagine anything!

Sing this song when you're:

• waiting in line, at the doctor's office, or at a restaurant
• bored during a car ride

Daniel and Katerina's families are at a restaurant. While they wait for their food to arrive, Daniel and Katerina play a guessing game with the objects on the table. Then they imagine that all the objects can come to life and sing! Soon the food arrives and it tastes *deeelicious*. Waiting is easier when you play, sing, and imagine!

Helpful hints for grown-ups:

• There are many ways to pass the time while you're waiting: playing a game, counting, singing, or imagining. Help your child brainstorm other things they can do.
• Waiting can be difficult, but it's also a great opportunity for your child to be creative. Encourage them to make up songs, draw a picture, and do other creative activities while waiting.
• Practice waiting for things at home. Cook foods with your child that take time, like cookies or veggie pizza. Understanding that things take time, and that patience often comes with rewards, will help your child stay calm while waiting.

Sometimes you need to play in a gentle way.

Sing this song when:

- you are playing with someone younger or smaller than you
- you are playing with a pet
- you are yelling or making a lot of noise while playing
- you or someone else is banging or throwing toys

Daniel and Margaret are playing on an obstacle course in the living room. Daniel wants to be loud and run fast, but then he remembers that he needs to be gentle with Margaret because she is smaller than him. He uses soft and gentle hands to help Margaret slowly cross the obstacle course. They both have fun playing gently!

Helpful hints for grown-ups:

• Tell your child that not everyone likes to play in the same way. Sometimes it's important to play slowly and gently so that no one is overwhelmed or accidentally hurt.
• Practice being gentle by using a toy. Show them how to touch it gently and how to talk in a soft voice.
• Remind your child that going too fast can lead to accidents and mistakes—like dropping something or bumping into someone else.
• Offer other ways for your child to let out their excitement and energy, like giving them time to run outside.

*It's almost time to stop,
so choose one more thing to do!
That was fun, but now it's done.*

Sing this song when:

- it's almost time to go home or it's almost time to eat
- your playdate is ending
- it feels hard to stop playing

It's time for Daniel to go home for dinner, but he doesn't want to stop playing with O the Owl. Dad Tiger tells Daniel to choose one more thing to do, so Daniel decides to pretend he is swimming as a sea turtle one more time! It is fun, and now Daniel feels ready to stop playing and go home.

Helpful hints for grown-ups:

• Giving your child one more thing to do makes them feel like they're in control of their own time.
• If you can, let your child know ahead of time when it's almost time to leave. That way, your child will be less likely to be caught off guard and get upset than when they're suddenly pulled away in the middle of playing.

Clean up, pick up, put away, clean up every day!

Sing this song when:

- you make a mess
- you're finished playing and need to put away your toys
- you need to make the house extra clean and tidy before an event

Daniel and O the Owl are playing together, but then Daniel realizes that his watch fell off. It's hard to look for the watch because his room is so messy with the toys everywhere. Once Daniel and O clean up the toys, it's much easier to find Daniel's watch!

Helpful hints for grown-ups:

• Singing a song is one way to turn a chore into a fun time. Cleaning up with other people is another way!

• Cleanup time feels overwhelming when there's a big mess. Breaking the job up into small chunks will make it feel easier. For example, you could ask your child to pick up all the toy cars first, followed by all the dolls, and so on.

• Have a designated place where everything should go. It's easier to clean up when your child knows where to put their toys. Your child will also be less likely to lose something the next time they play if there is a place for everything.

STAYING SAFE AND BEING SCARED

It's okay to feel scared sometimes. Being scared might help you stay safe. But if you pay attention and follow a plan, you can be safe without being scared, too.

Stop and listen to stay safe.

Sing this song when:
- you're playing outside
- you're crossing the street
- you're in a new place

Prince Tuesday, the crossing guard, takes Daniel's class on a safety walk through the neighborhood. They learn to stop at a stop sign, listen, and look both ways before crossing the street. There are many rules in the neighborhood to keep everyone safe!

Helpful hints for grown-ups:

• Tell your child that rules exist to keep people safe. Understanding why rules are important may make your child more willing to follow them.

• While you're walking, in a car, or on a bus, point out the different street signs that you see along the road. This activity will help children learn to look out for and pay attention to signs.

• Make sure to follow the safety rules yourself. Obey traffic signs, don't touch hot stoves, and avoid other behavior that go against the rules you're trying to teach your child.

See what it is.
You might feel better!

Sing this song when:

- you're visiting a new place
- you hear a mysterious sound
- you're afraid of the dark

Daniel is having his first sleepover at Prince Wednesday's castle. When they turn out the lights, Daniel sees a big scary shadow on the wall. They look closer . . . and discover that it's just a shadow of Mr. Lizard. Relieved, Daniel goes to bed. Sleepovers aren't scary—they're a lot of fun!

Helpful hints for grown-ups:

• Encourage your child to act out something that scares them. This will help your child feel in control of their fears and be less likely to feel helpless or powerless.

• Tell your child about the thing that scares them. If your child is scared of spiders, explain that spiders help get rid of other bugs and pests. When your child knows more, they will have more control over the fear.

 **Close your eyes and think of something happy!**

Sing this song when:
- you feel scared
- you feel nervous
- you feel sad

Boom! Daniel and O the Owl are playing inside, and the thunder is loud and scary outside. O closes his eyes and thinks about reading books. Daniel closes his eyes and thinks about playing with Tigey. Thinking of something happy makes them feel less scared of the thunder.

Helpful hints for grown-ups:

- Tell your child that it's okay to feel scared—grown-ups sometimes feel scared, too.
- Sometimes it's not possible to make a scary thing go away. That's why it's important to teach kids how to handle their fears by closing their eyes and thinking of something happy.
- Reassure your child that they are safe and loved!

Take a grown-up's hand,
follow the plan,
and you'll be safe!

Sing this song when:

• there is a storm or another emergency

• you're outside in a busy place or at night

There is a big storm coming to the neighborhood. The Tiger family has a plan to stay safe: Find a safe place inside, prepare an emergency supply kit, pack canned and dry food to eat, and have a safe place to sleep. By following the plan with his parents, Daniel is safe and sound during the storm.

Helpful hints for grown-ups:

• Make a safety plan and discuss it with your child. A safety plan usually includes a safe place to stay inside, an emergency supply kit, dry food and bottled water, and a safe place to sleep if you can't stay at home.
• During an emergency, try your best to keep to a routine. If possible, have your child go to sleep and wake up at the same time as usual. Continue traditions that your child is used to, like goodnight kisses.
• Your child may cry, become quiet, or cling to you during or after an emergency. They might even have potty accidents. Be patient with your child and don't forget to give them a lot of hugs.

Thank you, neighbor!

I hope you enjoyed learning the songs. Thank you for singing along with me! You can always change the words of the song to fit exactly how you're feeling . . . or you can even make up your own songs! What would you like to sing about? Is there a song that's special to you or your family? Ask your parents, caregivers, teachers, and friends to teach you their favorite song. It's so much fun to share songs and sing with people you love!

A note for grown-ups:

Remember that each and every child is different. Some hints and strategies in this book might work well with your child while others might not. That's okay! As Daniel Tiger sings, what's most important is to "Do your best. Your best is the best for you!"

INDEX